ANTA CLAWS
TH POLE
nta Claus
rth Pole
North Pole
St. Nickolas
North Pole
Mr. Santa
Father Chr
North Pole
rth Pole
Claws
Pole

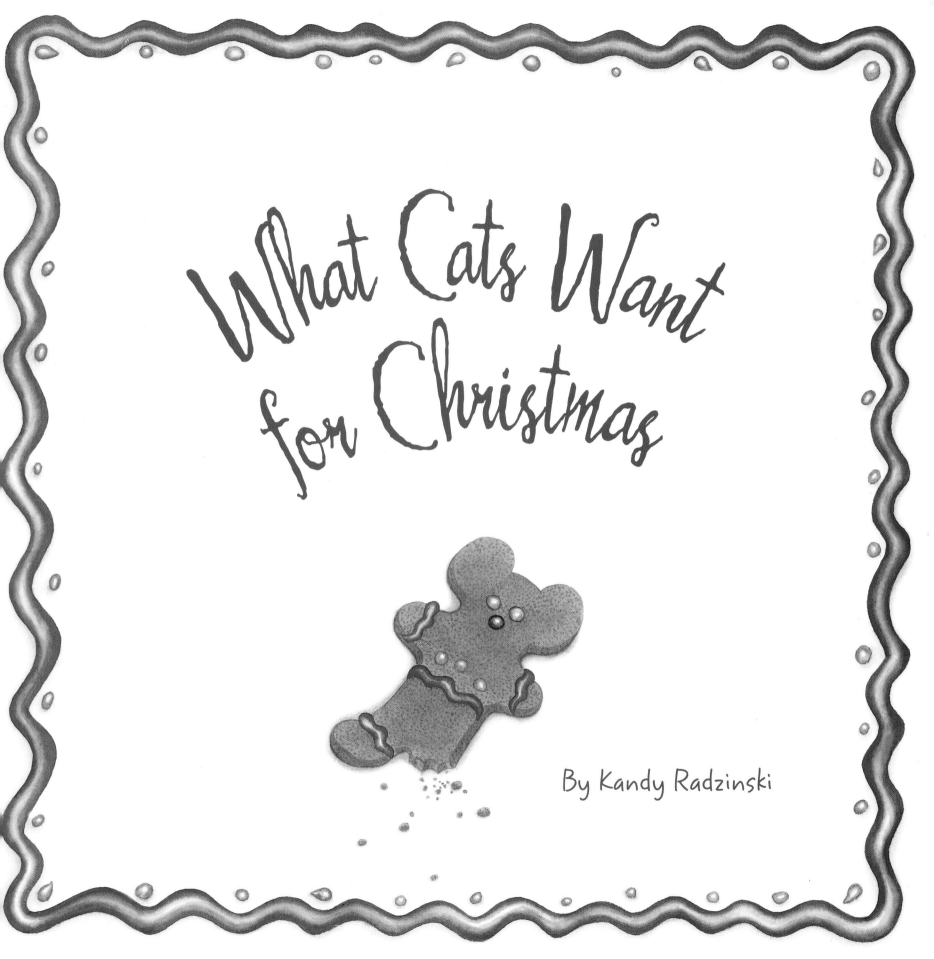

What Cats Want for Christmas

By Kandy Radzinski

Sleeping Bear Press™

310 North Main Street, Suite 300
Chelsea, MI 48118
www.sleepingbearpress.com

THOMSON
★
GALE™

© 2007 Thomson Gale, a part of the Thomson Corporation.

Thomson, Star Logo and Sleeping Bear Press are trademarks
and Gale is a registered trademark used herein under license.

Printed and bound in China.

10 9 8 7 6 5 4 3 2 1

Library of Congress Cataloging-in-Publication Data on file.

To my vet, Dr. D.C. Smith—
Thank you for taking such wonderful care of Brownie,
Rosie, Mr. Watson and Miss Mozie, and Kirby.
We appreciate you.

Kandy

Dear Santa,

I'd like a book on how to cook mice,
flamingo burritos, peacocks and rice,
sparrow spaghetti and pelican pie,
woodpecker pizza and pigeons on rye.

Love, Jade

Dear Santa,
I would like
a new, soft rug
made of Pomeranian
or pug.
Love, Kirby

Dear Santa,

I'd like a gingerbread house
and tucked inside—
a chocolate mouse
and fish eggs and snails...
and barbequed whales.

Love, Miss Kitty

Dear Santa,
I'd like to try
something new—
a totally different
hairdo.

Love, Rita

Dear Santa,
I want a partridge
in a pear tree,
a sparrow, a turkey,
and a chickadee.

Love, Sam

Dear Santa,
A brand new bed is what I'd love,
stuffed with feathers from
geese and doves.
A soft blanket of fowl wings,
a pillow of crows—
Oh, to wallow in plumage
from my head to my toes.

Love, Louie

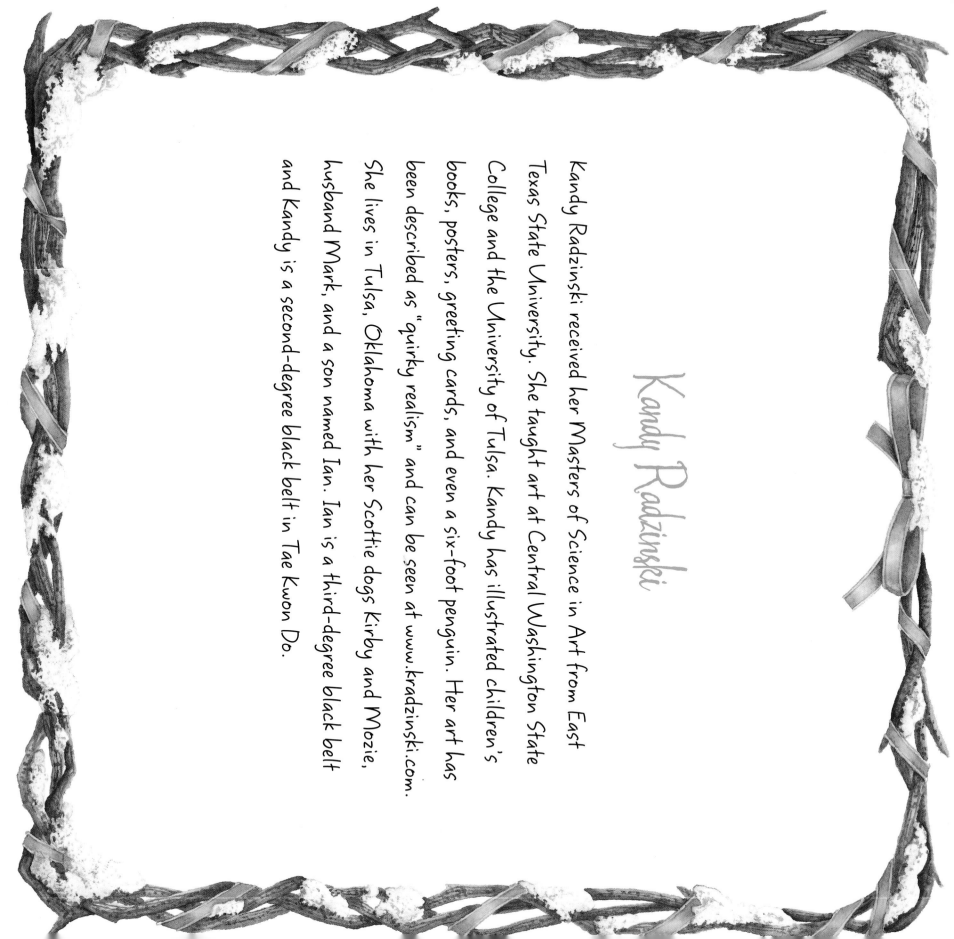

Kandy Radzinski

Kandy Radzinski received her Masters of Science in Art from East Texas State University. She taught art at Central Washington State College and the University of Tulsa. Kandy has illustrated children's books, posters, greeting cards, and even a six-foot penguin. Her art has been described as "quirky realism" and can be seen at www.kradzinski.com. She lives in Tulsa, Oklahoma with her Scottie dogs Kirby and Mozie, husband Mark, and a son named Ian. Ian is a third-degree black belt and Kandy is a second-degree black belt in Tae Kwon Do.

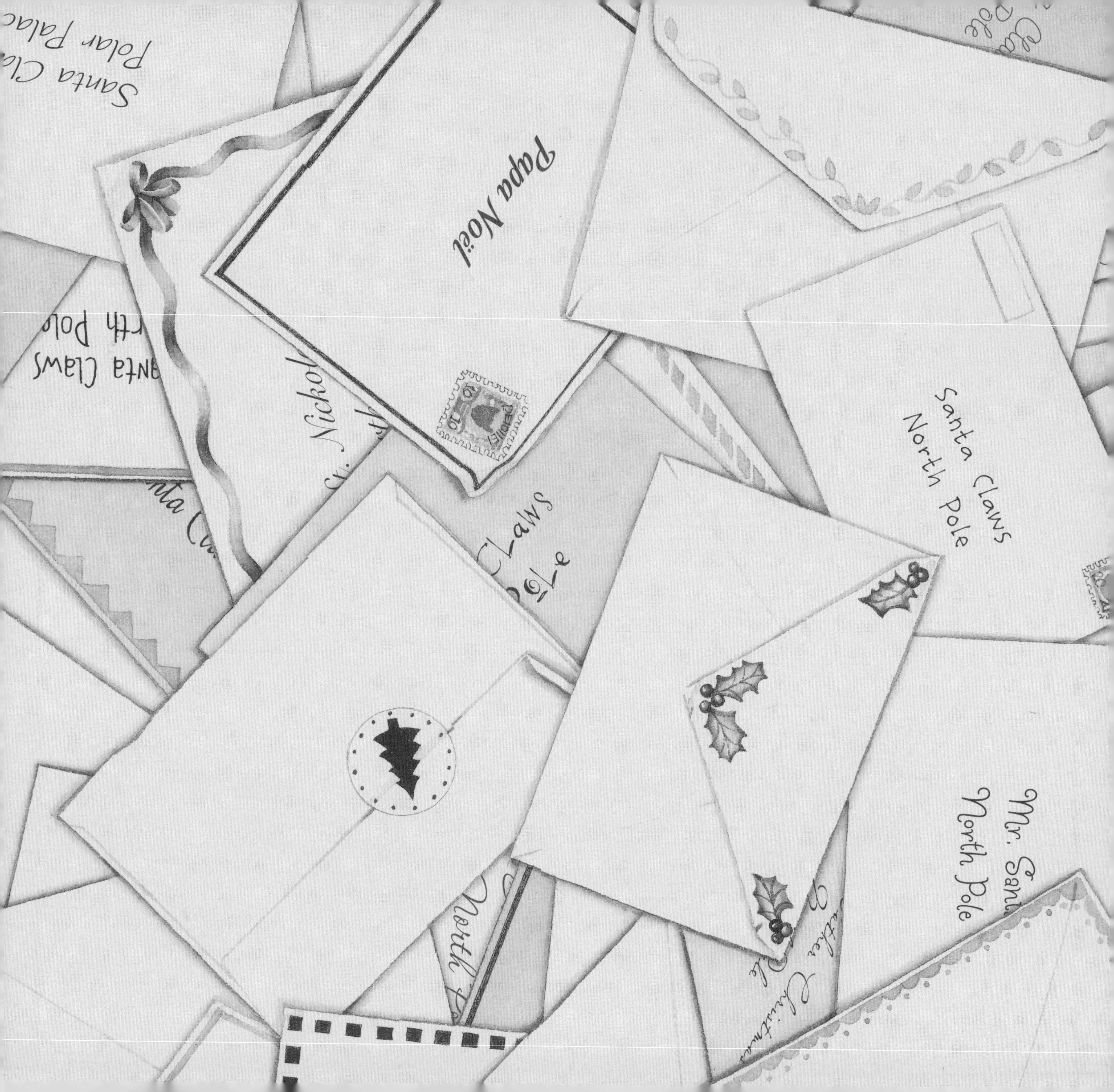
Papa Noël
Santa Claws
North Pole